OM NAMAH SHIVAY

First published in India in 2017 by Invincible Publishers

ISBN: 978-93-86148-38-4

Invincible Publishers
F-55, Sushant Lok II, Hong Kong Bazar Lane Sector 57, Gurgaon-122003

Opposite Kasturba Ashram, Radaur Distt Yamuna Nagar, Haryana- 135133

CHANDRA

#GoodWaliMorning

Dedicated to

Ravinder Singh (Sirji),

Whose quotes carved my life, and

Savi Sharma (didi),

Whose words touched my heart and my life.

Author's Note:

Everyone has a story. I too had a love story. But it was not just my story. But it is our story. The story that everyone would have in their lives. The story that everyone would feel in their life. It is not just a story, it is much above that.

This is about how #GoodWaliMorning quotes by Sirji on twitter carved my life. This is about what importance it held in my life. It is about love. It is about what it means to love.

It is a tale beaded from my life, our life. And what beaded it makes it special. Every morning a new page is added to this story.

Now, I just want you to put yourselves in the boots of "I" and enjoy reading your story.

Let your heart decide what you want to do. Let your brain figure out how.

Love? I always used to wonder what would love feel like. Would I also be in love? With someone? Would it be love at first sight? Or something else? I used to think that love at first sight would not be a right option. I wondered how could love happen at first sight? I heard some of my friends' debate on the topic- "Love or Lust" at the first sight? And all of it ended unanswered,

Which left me yet again with the same question- "what would love look like?" I never knew when I got the answer, but I knew that it was when I got you. An immense and an unreasonable pleasure joyfully played with my heart. My ears urged to hear more of you. My heart raced to your beats. I don't know what happened.

But there my mind said no. 'Your friend likes her. Not just friend, but your best friend likes her. What would you do if your heart says to go after someone who you think is not meant for you? But I just want to hear her.' You rose a conflict within me. For the first time I talked and questioned myself, and for someone else. Was I in love? Does Love look like this? Whatever it was, it was just beautiful, wordless, and expressionless and a piece full of peacefulness. Love is so lovely.

Today, probably I had my answer. My heart took over the turmoil and pushed my mind aside. I tried to control, behave, balance, but ended up falling in Love with you.

I rarely forget the times when life was unfair to me. I often forget when it was fair to me. Why being this unfair to life?

After all those years I am standing here, yet again. It is the 27th of January- the day I came to get my answer. Again my heart asks a question. "Why God why this to me? What sin I had been marked with that all this with me?"

I left her, I had a reason behind it, but she left me with many memories, I can't forget, what was the reason? Is love this way round? I slam the ground beneath me, sitting there alone. It was the place where I had first met her. Where I enjoyed her company for the very first time. Where she teased me like a kid for the very first time. Where my little cute love took birth for the very first time.

Every year I am used to come to the place and sit there all alone. First cursing my luck, then God and then laying there, setting my mind and my thoughts free. Then again coming to the same thought, convincing myself.

With all those painful memories, life has also gifted me with many unforgettable beautiful moments, some spellbound pleasures, something very beautiful, my Simran. And all those memories took birth here, at this right place. So, I must cherish this moment and remembering that beautiful past still shed a drop of sweet tear. The words that my heart can't say is being said by those tears. The tears that take birth in my eyes and end up on my lips. I, yet again, recall my dear Simran.

Simplicity has its own charm. Why complicate?

Sitanshu asked me to accompany me to have a walk. He seemed exited, I don't had any idea. He took me to the library, which was a place he kept distance from. Being a summer afternoon the place was quite quite. He said it was something special.

"Special? Would I also have something special, like my best friend has? I don't know who this special is, but she has a place to fill the 'special' place in Sudhanhu's life" I wonder. In my life…

No one seems to be present there until my eyes met yours. Sitanshu gives a smile that misses mine because I am deep stuck in those eyes of yours that spoke much of it even without exchanging any words.

"Simran"- she was the special whom Sitanshu wanted me to meet that afternoon. He accepts that he has some sort of likings for her. Simran, the lawn in front of the library, the afternoon- everything changed my view of life. Every moment spent there, today lies beautifully painted in my memory.

My heart raced. The blood in my veins pumped hard. My mind questioned myself. My eyes were busy reading your face, your cute smile. The simplicity it held behind itself. And to add to it were your melodious words. The beautiful charming day was a great turn in my life. It held many untold words that we never exchanged, but kept to our eyes and our hearts.

Do day dream! That's when your heart silently & candidly tells your mind what you want to do with your life.

"No. I can't. Sitanshu likes her. And after all, you don't know whether she also feels the same or not." My mind was disturbing my state of mind when the heart gained its command and started gaining its control over the topic.

"I am worth it. Whatever, she can be my friend as well. She may be liked by Sitanshu, maybe she likes Sitanshu too. But, it does not change anything. Every time I feel a rush when I see her." My heart was in full force and the debate was heavy on its side and then I intervened, 'Am I day dreaming?' I smile on myself. It is the first time I am day dreaming. I feel shy but admit it. I am really falling in love.

I remember the article where I had read day dreams are the most common phenomenon of love. It was difficult for me to convince myself but at last I was there. I had an idea.

'I am going to decide it tonight' I said to myself and laughed at the idea I had got. I was there, in confusion. How could I love someone whom my best friend loves already? And then my heart calmly explained my mind to express my feeling to her.

I don't expect anything from you. I just want you, to fill that vacant corner of my heart, the 'special' place deep within my heart which was unnoticed until I met you.

I smile again. I am day dreaming. My heart glitters.

I don't want to know my future. Why kill the sweet surprises of life before time? Why deal with shocks of life before time?

Walking with her alone, was for the first time in my relationship- probably our relationship. She is not worried walking with me alone. It seems as she believes and holds a place for me in her life. Finally I gather the courage to ask her.

"Do you believe in future?" I ended up making fun of myself. I asked a very absurd question. It was much harder than it seemed. "What have you done, yaar!"

Simran seemed confused, and then to ease her I laugh at my foolishness. She was gentle enough to smile.

"I mean, what would you do when you are in love with someone, you should not be?" I dared to ask at last.

"I would accept it. Of course, that is what I would do. And to answer about future, Arey! Yesterday is history, tomorrow is mystery. Today is a gift and so it is called Present. Cherish the moment yaar!" She smiled and pushed my hands away with hers.

It comforted me a lot. Finally, I convinced my mind, rather she convinced mine. She too had a place for me in her life. If not 'special', then at least 'yaar'.

I smiled the night when I was in bed with her memories that made me smile and toss and turn and then finally took me to a place where only me and her beautiful figure played hide-and-seek playfully. Her gentle touch. A world of lovely and precious dreams.

Don't depend on others to make difficult decisions of your life. You can't hold them responsible if they go wrong.

"Yeah! I can tell him and let him decide." I speak to myself. Ansh, a close friend of mine had sensed something going in my life that was different to me. He guessed it was love and that gave me a different glitter these days. By pressing me deep on the topic, now I was ready to tell him the truth. In our college, we shared many secrets including his love stories. It was the first time I was going to share mine.

"I am in great confusion. Yes, I know it owns very importance in my life and that I must decide something soon or I will create a mess." I ended my story with these last few words. He kept listening and absorbing everything calmly. At last a smile broke on his face.

"You should go for it. Don't fear, *aakhir Sitanshu tera yaar hai.* He is your friend he'll understand your feelings." We hugged and he departed.

Now, my heart getting another one on its side had the battle on its side. Now, every day seemed to be full of new surprises and every evening the time to share those secrets to Ansh. By every passing day, Simran became a closer friend of mine. Yes we defined our relationship in words with friendship, but deep within it meant something else, something special. It was all going great until I regretted speaking my heart out.

Simran came to me and said it was all going to end. Someone asked her to keep distance from me.

Only your loved ones can hurt you. You haven't given that right to others.

It was after many days that I could not sleep well. The memories of Simran played with my dreams well to offer me a sound sleep. But, today was different. There was no Ansh to hear my heart out, nor was my dream girl to conceive my heart. I was left all alone. I could not control myself, nor were my eyes able to control my tears until Sitanshu came.

He asked me for a walk, which could be some refreshment. I took time to be prepared to face him amidst all that I had gone through. He took me to the very lawn. Today, there was no Simran waiting for us, rather Ansh and a few more close friends of me and Sitanshu. The joined us and then began the most terrible part of my story.

Sitanshu remained silent for all but I could feel his fain. On the other hand I had to feel the pain of those words that my closest friends spoke to me. "Betrayal! How could you do this? How could you think of breaking them apart, when you knew Sitanshu liked Simran?" This line had made the worse impact on me and I could hardly hold back my emotions. To keep my tears from falling I didn't spoke a word.

I knew what it all meant. "Time will answer all your questions." It was all that I could dare to speak. The silence that was broken on Ansh made me feel even worse. I knew it hurts the most when someone hurts you, you never thought would hurt you.

When you are punished for a crime you didn't do, the brain starts believing I would have better done that crime. But that is when you have to hear your heart.

I sat there in my bed. It was midnight. I could not sleep. The evening had torn me apart. Every words of my friends, Ansh, Simran, now and then bounced in my ears. It felt as if I was accused of something I never did.

I remembered how, every day, I would ask about Sitanshu from Simran, the very first question of our conversation was always about him. But then I was accused of trying to separate them. I always kept a line of separation between our relationship so that it may not separate Sitanshu and here again I was blamed. Whatever I felt in heart, I never spoke it out to her to keep that line maintained.

For a moment I thought I should have done so. And the other moment my heart burst on my mind. "How could you even think of it?" And then it started convincing me, "Love! You loved Simran. You respected Sitanshu. And for both of them to be well and happy, you must sacrifice. Probably Simran would have also accepted the truth that I am not meant to be a part of her life."

They were not pleased with all that they ended up hardly scolding and ending up everything with Simran. It was a great shock for her. She was hard hit in her heart.

The very day, she rushed to the hospital. All her tears had roused her to a high fever.

The most difficult time of your life can shape the rest of your life. Fight!

She threw my hands with that intensity that it hurt badly smashing the bench. I followed Simran to the hospital. Her sad face had turned out the greatest pain for me that time. Even though, I was to keep distance from her, this was not the time. I held her back, this time her head. I slammed my forehead against her. This was the first time we were that close. I could read her eyes, her tears dipped into mine. Now they were mine too. "Don't worry. I will make everything okay. I promise." These were the only words I could speak before I myself lose my control. Seeing in that state of mind held my heart hard. I could not see her this way.

With her high fever, she was admitted in the hospital. I was to do something for her. The only way out was to get to the hospital and make her feel that she had someone by her side. But for that I would have to be with her. It would raise another question against me from my friends. It would also affect Simran's relation with Sitanshu. And there I was again in between the conflict of my mind and my heart. My mind said no while the heart said to go.

It was probably the most difficult situation and to help me out of it was no Ansh and no other friends. And my heart was not even going to risk it again with Ansh or any other.

Then keeping all other thoughts aside, it was time for me to go. I had my promise to keep. I chose to be by her side.

I would love to believe in destiny. But then I wouldn't get up from my bed for destiny will take care of everything for me.

I didn't have the very idea that what was going to happen next. Either I would lose my friendship, or my love, or worse, both. Yes I believed in destiny. I knew I was destined to face all this. But then this #GoodWaliMorning quote shaped my life.

"I just want you to remember me when you are alone, so that I may help you with that loneliness. I just want you to remember me when you are sad, so that I may share that sadness with you. I just want you to remember me when you are depressed, so that I may share the load that your heart has to carry, so that I may lighten your heart. I want you to remember me when you shed a tear, so that I may break a smile on your lips from the tear drop. I just want this from you and nothing else." I sat by her side, holding her hands in mine. Her hands feel hot against my cold palm. She is in sleep with her high temperature when my cold tears fall on her forehead. I don't know even if she hears me but I continue, "I am here and I promise I would always be by your side, in all the ups and downs of your life."

I had decided to face everyone and was sitting there with my love. Whatever, I was destined to, I was going to face with all my efforts.

'In "our" life Mr.' she smiles and intertwines our hands together. She broke a smile on my face from those painful tears.

There is a kid in all of us. Let's not let that kid die.

"It's you." Her reply amazes me. I had asked her about her favorite dish and never expected such an answer.

We were in our Wednesday-talks when I chose to ask our favorites.

"What? I asked your favorite dish that you would love to eat?" I asked in astonishment.

"Yes, I answered it well. It is you." She smiled and said which left me more confused.

"So how are you going to eat me?" I asked playfully.

She doesn't need words to answer. She comes closer to me and places her hands on mine. She bends towards me and I feel that gentle and tender kiss on my cheeks. It leaves me spellbound, but there I fell the tenderness of it, the purity in it. I do nothing in response but smile with her child-like act. Now we feel like little kids playing and enjoying. We cherish that beautiful moment together.

She tickles my nose and asks, "Aren't you going to reply? Or are you still not done with your answer?" that mischievous smile of hers again fills me with immense joy. By doing such small thing she gave me those happiness which meant a lot for me.

I answer her with the same tenderness and enjoy our company in the lap of nature without exchanging any further words.

Value the little things we have got without asking for them. There are so many of us who never got them.

This time, time had been great with me. I had accepted that I had someone that held the 'special' place in my heart. We started sharing everything together.

"I am sorry, but I really took Sitanshu from your life. I never wanted it, but…"one day I opened my heart out. Every night I used to think about Sitanshu when I thought Simran. It felt hard to be so hard to be your friend. But the love acts such, it makes you do many things that you never thought you would.

"No, it's not your fault. I too feel sorry but you know, he is so. He never came to me after that." She too shared what she felt. Her words reflected the sadness that was hidden behind it, "I thought if he held something for me, he would certainly come. But…" It felt like she still regretted Sitanshu. Yes, it was what I would have not loved. But still I was there with my love. "But, I have someone special by my side. My best friend.

To comfort my dynamic state of my mind was here beautiful smile. She looked deep in my eyes. I found a reflection of myself in hers. It felt nice to have her beside me. It felt nice to have that truthfulness with me. It felt nice to have that faith with me. It felt nice to have that smile beside me. She, yet again, had deepened her place in my heart. The place that had been untouched till then.

The fear of losing your best friend should not be a reason behind not proposing her.

She does not even notices me. She ignores me for I am very late on our Wednesday-talk. Seeing her cute face, I could not hold back my laughter. Her cheeks are glowing crimson. I went to her and sat near her. She turns her head away. That child-like behavior again makes me smile.

"What happened to my cute little angel?" I ask teasing even though I know the answer very well. For a moment when I get no reply, I took out the rose that I had brought with me but had not shown Simran. I held it in front of her. She does not reply but bends forward to take the rose from me.

"I was caught in a question" I replied taking my hand behind so that she may not get it.

"Then?" She bends again.

"The question was- 'what is the difference between me and Sitanshu?' And I could not get the answer." I replied, again taking my rose behind so that she could not get hold of it.

"Then?" She again bent.

"I want my answer." I said taking the rose behind my back. She had come close enough for me. She lays her head in my lap and says, "Quite simple. I respect him but love you."

I present the rose to my best friend, "I love you too, dear."

The hard skills can be taught. The small skills can only be learned.

I had always had a great interest in literature. It always attracted me and I was much influenced by it. Once I wrote a small poem for the one who attracted me more than literature.

It was about a lover who was going to leave her beloved and to go on for a long journey ahead. In fact, I had just finished the novel "Everyone Has A story" by my favorite author. And so the topic reflected one of its important incident.

I read the poem for her when we were departing one evening. I tried just to make her a little worried with the poem. It reflected truly a difficult scene for the beloved and the way I read, it made clear whom I was referring with lover and the beloved.

"Waise to poora samagh me nahi ayo, par shayad theme samagh gaye. Aur Bye! Bye, hum nahi bolte dear- itna Jaldi kaise chor denge aapko, haan?"

I held great love for my poems, but from that evening I came to know I held something that was more lovable to me. It was her words, it was the cute and the true feelings, the instant replies of her. It was all that made me mad for her. I liked to play with words and yes I had great skills in that, but then I loved being played in her words, in her beautiful words. I wanted to learn her, that, small skill which meant a lot for me, but then I was there, immersed in the depths of her words.

The most satisfying happiness comes from making others happy.

We were chatting on WhatsApp when she suddenly wrote 'baad me baat krte h'.

'Why? What happened?' I asked. No reply.

'Where are you now?' I became worried because there was no reply. One thing that comforted me was that my messages were double-ticked in blue and her last seen changed every few minutes. Yes, she was checking my messages, but why was she not replying?

I started typing another message when I remembered that a few minutes ago when she had called me to tell something, I had disconnected it and rather chose him texting. I thought probably she was just upset with that. And so I again typed back, 'Sorry dear. ☹'

The next moment I had a call from her, "Niche aiye (come down)" She was laughing her heart out which left me more confused.

She held me by my hand and took me to the Gurudwara, a few steps away from our hostel. She was still smiling and was not ready to answer why she had brought me here.

"Let's serve in this Langar. It would be fun, you know!" she smiled as we stepped together in the Gurudwara. That really gave us great satisfaction as well as much peace. These small things were there in Simran which made her special from others. She held the air whose fragrance held me.

Sometimes we need to distance ourselves from them in order to come closer to them.

Our semesters were going to begin the next day. This Sunday when we met, the exams and its preparations were the main concern in our conversation. And then she suddenly broke a huge load on me, probably on us. She suggested that we should meet for the period when the exams were going on, which meant for two weeks. Two weeks were much more to control. Oh!

I felt sudden desire to meet her. It's been days that I saw her or heard her only for the smilies that we used to share after the exams. And that desire grew much larger in a few moments. I threw my books away and jumped on my bed. I jumped on my feet the other moment, 'I can go to the lawn'. The lawn in front of the library. It was the place that held many of our conversations, many of our secret lovely teasy talks.

'How come you be here?' I ask in astonishment when I see Simran present there. I show if her being present there disturbs me but I am pleased from inside.

'I may ask the same question?' she replies. Her voice seems more pleasant than ever. It quenched my thirst to hear her. 'Okay! I am going.' I sighed and turned to return. 'Waise, are you prepared for your next exam?' She stops me.

The beauty of her lips quench the thirst of mine. I had missed her much in that week and she too certainly had. But the moment fills all. For seconds, or minutes we enjoy each other, together.

On some day let's be selfish for somebody else's happiness.

"It's something special for my special one." I smile and say. I had called her to the garden that evening before going to attend our evening left-out lessons in the collage. She feels a little surprise for I had never before called her, not in the evening.

"Why?" she extended that why which made that why look more than just lovely. She is extremely talented in those things.

"I scored highest in our batch. Isn't it a day to celebrate?" excitement overjoyed my words. But then, I got a very different reaction. Simran held the wrist watch that I had just gifted her with a frowned face. She did not even smile, nor did she spoke anything. She just said the words, "I know you are happy when you see me smile. But have you ever thought of me?" These words of hers penetrated deep within my heart. The things we do being unselfish, can they be this Selfish when seen from a different point of view.

That mistake of mine made me wonder the whole night and the next day,

"Wooooow! You look wonderful" she exclaimed, seeing me in my new attire. I held my favorite cone in my hand. I always used to bring another one for her, but today, this ice cream meant only for me.

"Where's mine?" Simran is excited. "Someday let me be a little selfish dear!" I touch her cheeks. She is looking cute with that anger and cream on her cheeks.

Losing cool has never solved any problem. Never ever.

"I am not going to take anything. Just that. And I'm going." Simran barked at me but heartily she felt nice.

"I would send it with someone else." I shouted back when she had gone a few distance from me. I wanted her to gift her my favorite chocolate- Silk. Even though it was my favorite, I knew Simran would also like it. Her birthday was also in a day and two so she had the point that she should be gifted then.

As I saw her entering the hostel gate, an idea struck me, someone came out of the gate at the same moment. Simran waited for a moment to hug her and then smashed her with her bag. Probably she had teased her. She was Anjali, Simran's good friend these days. Anjali, Priya and Simran always used to be together.

"For the three musketeers. In fact, it's my favorite and I wouldn't have liked it to gift you. But take it, yaar." I smiled handing over the Silk to Anjali.

"Are you sure, for all three?" Anjali teased. I smiled and nodded. I had always liked their friendship.

"I can't take this. Get it back." Anjali said with a frowned face. "Simran says that you have given this to me, so either I should through those chocolates away our friendship."

"Get it to me." I took the three 'Silks' from her, "Say her to check the dustbin of your college gate."

When wrong, saying sorry is so simple. But our ego makes us take the difficult route of finding excuses.

"Don't do this to her. She is not prepared for it. She is much more than a sorry to that." Anjali tries to convince me but I am unmoved. It's been two or three days that I talked her. After what Anjali had told me, I only tried to ignore her and never spoke a word to her.

"She had been crying all the night. Don't be that cruel to her." Anjali said.

'To her? I am being cruel to myself. Don't you know what am I facing? Even now how am I holding my tears?' I speak to myself. I want to her to listen me but then 'She is not my Simran who could listen all that my heart said, even without words.' It had been much hard for me.

"She, even, brought back the chocolates that you threw, from the dustbin. She keeps it to her chest and cries in deep pain."

I was struck. 'What is she saying? Has she really brought it back from the dustbin? Does she care me this much? Oh! My dear Simran!' I yell at myself and ran away from that point. My heart could not bear more.

We always used to fight so as to make it easy to depart from our talks, but it lasted only for a few moments. We always turned and smiled while our paths changed. But this time, 'Why didn't we turn back to smile? Why tears had took the place of the cute smile?

Our passion has immense power to change our lives. Only if we are willing to unleash it.

"The smiles of my killing heart."

It touches my heart
And always reminds its past
It plays in my brain
And blossoms with pain

It rushes with blood
And brings the flood
That borns in my eyes
And touches me twice

Through my nose and lips
And then my mind flips
As you used to do
For these are memories of you

The words spoken by my tear
That only you can hear
Which my heart speaks
And your presence it seeks

Putting those beautiful memories beside
It kills me from inside
Though, I give a smile too
Because it always reminds of you
Even if it kills me for you.

Your passion is the balm for the daily aches of life.

"Sorry to make you cry
But do you know why
Oh! Whatever it be
Let it be mistake by me

Sorry but a question I want to ask
After my such hurting task
Do you still care?
And do you still love?

Sorry, I heard you cry
Which made me shy
But did you ever think?
How deep I was sink!

Sorry but I have to say
For all, I too had to pay
I wanted to cry
But my eyes were dry

And all the efforts
My heart had to make
And all the loads
Were left on my heart's stake

Sorry, but I don't want to lose you this way
And end our precious hours this way
Sorry dear, but I have to say this
But I really missed you lovely lovely kiss☺"

*Go beyond the excuses and answer the question-
how bad you want it?*

It is Simran's birth day. We both know that she is not going to celebrate. 'But why don't you go and wish her?' My heart says.

'But she could have also come. I gifted her the present with such love, and she made it threw in the dustbin.'

'Also did she took that out for herself.' My heart objects. 'Why do I need to justify it to myself?' My brain is trying to convince itself that it is correct. 'But is it so?' *"I must be true to myself!"* I speak out loud in my bedroom. This morning had been the most difficult one.

She is there. I can see her in the lawn. She is sitting there alone, probably celebrating her birthday with my memories as I had been doing in my dreams. I walk upto her from her back. I want her to surprise.

"Happy Birthday Dear!" I hissed in her ear softly kissing her. She jumps. The smile that comes from her tears made me to hold her. I hug her tight. She does the same in response.

"So pleased to hug my little angel!" I exclaimed.

"This is the best birthday present I ever got." She spoke lightly in my ear.

We sat there enjoying the best moment of our life. This place has always been the place which broke new surprises for us every new day.

She sits beside me holding my hands, and rests her head on my shoulder. In my eyes she can easily read, "Sorry!"

Truth doesn't have multiple versions; it has just one. There can be multiple perspectives to look at that one truth.

"No, not this time. I have some important assignments to finish" it was very difficult for us to face each other. Ansh had come upto my room and was asking me to accompany for a walk. It was also very difficult for him to take the first step and it could be easily seen in his discomfort.

"Please" he tried to convince. 'What? Please? What had happened to you that day? Not even a single word you spoke. And I am not going to forgive you for that which you did to me' my mind spoke in fury.

But in my words I spoke something else, "Okay! Whatever." We met Sitanshu outside our gate as we stepped together. It made me more uncomfortable as I saw him. He was waiting for us. As he joined me, it reminded me of the past. How deeply had they hurt!

"I am here just to ask you something." Sitanshu started with his face sunk, "Sorry" he said facing me. "Shouldn't we forget everything and again be the best-friends?"

'I had someone who took that best-friend place after you. And how could you expect me to forget everything after all this you did not one to me, but Simran?' My mind yelled but I spoke nothing.

"The truth was just one, you loved Simran. And that does not change even if we be or not be friends. From my perspective, you were a culprit, but it was not until today that I realised your view." He understood, "Sorry..."

Ego can kill everything. Kill ego first.

'Should I really forgive him?' my mind asked.

'At least he understood my way. He too was hurt that day.' Why the heart does always says the opposite of mind? Can't they be convinced at a same thought?

'And Sitanshu had no mistake in doing so. He was not aware of everything. But the mistake was by Ansh's side.'

"Okay! But you would have to do something for me." I spoke. I had something in my mind that would be helpful for all.

"I am ready." Sitanshu smiled. He seemed happy but was still uncomfortable.

"Why are you feeling so tensed? I am not going to ask Simran." I teased to comfort him, "Rather, I am going to make you two up. Again." I surprised him. "You would have to be normal with Simran."

It was the correct opportunity to put all the beads together. I remember Simran once telling, "How good it would have been, had it be with all of us together- me, you, and Sitanshu." I had understood that I had a place in her life but there was another for Sitanshu. The place I never saw, I never seek. But his absence leaves the place vacant which, in some corner of her heart, hurts Simran. And anything that hurts her, hurts me too, even if I…

Go catch her up!" I teased again and we all burst into laughter. It was such a long time that we all had enjoyed together.

Only when you earned it, you experience an unparalleled joy.

"In the name of our friendship" we all raised our glasses and cheered. Even though there was Ganne-ka-juise in place of wine in our glasses, it added more fun to our reunion.

It was a very long time after that Sitanshu, Simran, and I were celebrating together, probably the first time after I met her. It was such a fun. We had first invited Ansh and then told him, "Arey! Kabab me haddi kyun banega? Chor de!" It was a great fun making fun of him. And the best part of friendship is that, "Real friends don't get offended when you insult them. They smile and call you something even more offensive."

"Chal bata. What made you love Simran, love at first sight?" Sitanshu left the first bomb on me. I was not prepared for such a question and even without any pre-warning!

"I…I just…" I could not answer the question. I did not love Simran for any reason. Love needs no reason, it just happens. And when it happens, there is no time to think for the reasons. There is no need, you just need to life that beautiful love. And cherish every moment of that love.

"Okay, first you tell me the reason." I left his thread with himself. "Do you had any reason?" I asked him even though I knew that Simran was present there and it would make her feel awkward.

"Yeah! I had."

If you truly consider me to be your friend, expect me to point out flaws in you as & when I see. Don't expect fake praises.

"God is wonderful. How could he send someone with such a voice? Your voice is really very pleasant." Sitanshu complimented.

The evening after such a funny day was delightful. Simran had just sung a song to make our reunion more wonderful. Even though she sung, but it was due to our force. I knew she had not sung her whole-heartedly. I knew she had more than this to make the atmosphere delighted, but she did not show up all.

I kept silent, my face sunk and eyes closed. I wanted Simran to enjoy this evening with her open heart, filled with love and only love.

"What happened? Why don't you say anything?" Sitanshu asked me after few moments as he noticed me. "Didn't you like the song?"

Simran had been listening to us but chose to just keep watching.

"Nothing. I just didn't like the one who was singing. I love my Simran, who is always charming and never does anything with her half-heart." I explained and smiled to dismiss what I had just said.

"Tu bhi paagal hi hai yaar" Sitanshu said and we all laughed together.

Later, when Sitanshu left us, Simran asked a question, "Really, what makes you love me so much?"

Her question left me surprised. "Probably because you always have some questions and queries like this one?" We both laughed. We both knew the answer.

Imaginations have so much potential. Imagine!

"What are you thinking?"

She did not reply. We were sitting in the same lawn on one of our Wednesday-talks. For a moment we all became silent. She was probably thinking something but what?

"Kuch nahi." She replied, and her cute voice made me tease her.

"Please. Say once again what you just said. Aww it was so cute… Chota baua." I tease her in a kid's voice.

"Oh! Don't disturb me. I am thinking, what would it feel like when in place of you Ansh would have been sitting her with me? In this silence, in this privacy."

'Oh hell. She is teasing me on the other part.' A part of myself feels jealous and the other part, "Then? What do imagine after that?"

"I come closer to her and he holds me by my waist" she says coming closer to me and I follow, "Then? What more do you think?"

"I rest my heads on his shoulder and…" Simran rests her head on my shoulder.

"And what next?" I ask in her ear slowly.

"And then he kisses my neck and goes moving up." Her voice too has gone low. She imagines and I follow. Our eyes are closed by now.

"And what next do you imagine?"

"Oh ho! Why are you interviewing me and Ansh between such things?" She bump off in a loud voice.

Not to make a choice is also a choice.

"What would you chose? Love or passion?" Her innocent questions have always made me feel more to spend with her.

I had been telling her about the poem that I had sung for her that day and she turned the scene upon me by saying, "I don't speak bye." It was one of my favorite stories, "Everyone Has A Story" After hearing that the lover had left the beloved behind for his passion of travelling, she had come up with that innocent question.

I am in no mood to answer the little girl with the same innocence with that she asked me the question. But I want her to ask more of that innocence, so I think of confusing her.

"It is a difficult question for me. I think." I pause to make the drama more realistic.

"I love my passion which is my love." I try to circle out the whole thing.

Simran makes a cute face. She is blushing from inside, I know.

"Why not putting my love in my passion? Why not I bind you in some of my works?"

"In some of your work?" The innocence again turns up in front of me. I smile.

"May be someday I would make you immortal in my best work. Maybe I would tell the world about my special one. Someday, I would."

Don't make promises that you cannot keep.
Avoid breaking hearts.

"Promise me." Her angry face always makes me smile.

"Why would I, when I don't want?" I object. Simran is pressing me to promise her that I am not going to leave her.

I am in a mood to make her angrier, to get more beauty and innocence bush in front of me.

"Why don't you want to want to promise just this simple thing?" And yes there came the innocent question I wanted.

"Why caring the 'just simple thing'?" I asked to add to her anger.

"Okay! I am done. You say this just simple thing?" She bumped.

"I didn't say that. You were the first to define it like that." I laugh at her move.

"Okay! Do not promise. In fact, go and promise it to someone else. That would be not a simple thing for you, haan?" Simran went dumb after saying all. She behaved like a little kid and this time I had the reason to make her happy again. It would be fun again.

"My dear," I begin in a very romantic tone, "Why don't you suggest me some beautiful girls?" I laugh loud. It makes Simran turn her face away.

"Okay! Okay! My dear Simran. I am ready to promise. I certainly would. For my little angel, I would never leave my dream girl alone, not for this life I promise." I smile, "May the next life would bring someone more beautiful." We laugh out together.

Take your chance today. In future, you don't want to repent not taking them when you had the opportunity.

"Couldn't you make it a little later, Sirji?" I spoke in irritation.

It was a pleasant Sunday morning when I was woken by the #GoodWaliMorning quote of Ravin sir. But I could not help me for having a nap again for these quotes held a great importance in my life. I checked the tweet when my eyes fell on another GoodWaliMorning tweet of him.

'Take my chance today? Should Me?' it was no more than we were going to leave our college behind and the college counseling had already begun. I knew we had very less time left together. 'Am I going to ask her? When?' Whatever I had to do, it was to be done soon. Yes, I am going to ask her today.

"Where were you by now?" I asked Simran. She was smiling when she came late to meet me that morning.

"Sitanshu just stopped me. He had something to say." Simran replied, "Sorry, he said."

The happiness on her face made me to think. I knew she had never made me wait any time before, not for someone else. Probably she held something with her that she never dared to show up, deep in her heart.

"Simran, you have got something with you. Take your chance today. In future, you don't want to repent not taking them when you had the opportunity." When I saw her in confusion I changed the topic,

"Why don't we have a walk today? We would also make Sitanshu with us. It would be fun."

Think positive. More so, when the environment around us is so negative.

"I won't be coming today. I am not feeling well. Probably some sleeping bug." We smiled and hung up.

It is Wednesday morning. I have probably lied her for the first time. Not the sleeping bug, but a non-sleeping bug certainly would have kept me from the lie. I could not have a good sleep these nights. My mind went wandering and eyes they were glued to the ceiling above.

That I could not ask her what I wanted. I was well prepared to ask her about us, our future. But then, there was something that stopped me that day. But yet, I never repent that nor would I do in future. I knew what I was doing. I knew there was something that Simran never spoke me. I knew that, that someone was more important than me. He held the place in heart that I could not. Simran had offered it to him, very earlier.

"You said you were going to sleep." Someone tapped me from behind. I recognized the voice and the touch in one go.

"Hum… I just…" I did not except her. "Nothing." I dismissed. Simran was there with Sitanshu.

It left me a little sad. But then, I knew it was what I wanted. I was to keep my promise and that I was keeping well.

'I would never leave you alone. Never ever. You would always live with the one You Love.'

If you are left with nothing else to lose, you are back at an advantage point.

I have done a mistake
That you should not make
I left everything for you
You should not do too

You must go with him, together
For he is none another
But the one you more love
And thus he is all above

For you love him more
And I love you by my heart core
So I won't stop you
And won't ask even a questions few

Even if you are with him, and my heart roasts
When I see your happiness, my heart boasts.

Relationships work when we focus on what to give to it and not just what we take from it.

"You are not coming? Why?" Simran types back.

I had just informed her that I would not be able to accompany them this evening. I had prepared the plan to hang around this Sunday evening together- Simran, Sitanshu and me.

"Ltl bsy. Tlk 2 u latr." I replied. It was nice that she had not called. It was difficult for me to even speak. My heart was choked with words that I was not able to speak.

"Maybe we should cancel the program then." She responded with a sad smiley.

"No. You guys enjoy should enjoy." I wrote and went offline. 'Why is it always so difficult?'

"Please come down here. Only for a moment" says Simran from the other side. She had called me and her pleasant voice could not be objected by me.

There is no one around. The street below is dark only for the little light provided from the street lamps that light the main road. The college gate can be seen in far. But no one near it. She had told me to wait there.

"If it's her play again, I'm not going to leave her." I spoke with the little left energy with me.

"First, catch me dear." I can feel the kiss as she hugged me. "You look cute and dumb!"

Tears roll down my eyes. She wipes them away and kissed again. 'It feels light with her, but not right?'

Often the easy task appears to be the right task, even when it's not.

'What should I do?' I speak out loud as I get up from my dreams. It is midnight and I am unable to sleep.

Something is there that hurts me. Something that stops me. I know that I too hold a little place in her heart. The place that no one can ever take from me. But that does not make to let things go on their own.

Sometimes things take such a turn that it makes you take turn with that thing. It seems the best you can do with that. The easiest looks the best.

'Why was she there to wipe out my tears? Why was she there to kiss me when I wanted her not to?'

Was it because the fact that Sitanshu had left her behind once? Was is that she had forgiven him but could not forgotten what he did?

Yes it was true that Sitanshu had once left her. Even though, he was now there for her, who knows that he would be there in the future too?

"Someday she must not regret the choice she made. Someday she must not think about "the road not taken."

But what was the road she was going to take. I knew, Simran herself cannot decide that.

"I have my promise to keep. Even if sometimes Sitanshu is not there for her, I always will be. Even if I make her chose Sitanshu, I always will be there for her.

Difficult challenges are also a great a great opportunities to prove yourself.

My life was going in such a direction I never wanted. For some days I tried to run from it, then I knew that it's like your shadow. The more you ignore those situations, the darker it begins.

Nothing was going "well" in our life. Simran tried to contact me but at the same time I saw myself going to be that "Kabab me haddi" between Simran and Sitanshu.

Then I tried to gulp everything. Then I was there, sitting outside my room, on the stairs. It was the only place left for me. I could see my dear Simran from there, but she was not there to notice me.

The thing that I gulped choked me. I could not speak what I wanted to. It felt like…

I coughed, coughed, and coughed. I had the problem that doctors said was due to some stress or allergy. The former seemed more correct that situation.

I could not breathe. My nose were chocked. I stood and then fell. Everything around seemed vanishing.

Simran came to me. She says, "I may not be yours. But you certainly be mine. An essential part of my life that would live until me." She held her hands forward when Sitanshu woke me up.

I don't know when I slept on my bed. I don't know what happened with me then. But I knew I had a challenge ahead. I was to prove me and my love by making Sitanshu fall in love with her.

Be a human enough to own up your own sins.

"Sometimes they don't" I spilled those words with my voice filled with anger as well as pain.

Sitanshu sat in front of me in the café. I had asked him the reason he left Simran behind. Hearing his reply that, "I heard my friends, my mind. They always seem right." I was left with great pain.

"They do but they are not always." I said calmly again.

"What do you mean?"

"I mean, there is something that Simran holds of you till now. She holds a place in her heart that belongs to you and only you."

"What are you talking about?" He is confused hearing those words.

"I mean that you must be with her. You must be the one you used to be. You must know and value what you have got. It is much more than this. You own your sins." I wait for a moments and then continue. My eyes are wet. It is very difficult to open up everything in front of me. But it feels right.

"I mean that I was on the wrong point loving her. Maybe the truth cannot be changed, but you are the one who can change her life." I paused to let him absorb everything I spoke.

Sitanshu knew what I was speaking and respected my feelings. He did not ask anything else. "I own mine." I said and left the café.

There's no substitute for nostalgia. You know you were there, in that moment, which today has become a memory.

I left the café. I never turned back to see him. Probably to hide the words that my heart spoke. The tears that rolled down my eyes. But there was no Simran to wipe them. To break a smile on that sad face. That single decision changed my life.

I never heard her pleasant voice again, nor did she heard mine. It took time for Simran to overcome, I know, but she did. She was with her love. And I used to see them change in their new profile photos. I had left behind everything, my love, my life.

But the lawn and my passion never left me. I still remember every moment spent with her. The tenderness of her hands when she held it like a child in that hospital. The fingers that were not letting mine to go. I still remember the smile that made me smile even in dreams.

I still have dreams of her, but then, I never repent them. I love her in those dreams too. Not all my dreams come true, but that will not stop me from dreaming. Her voice still echoes in my ears, in my heart. She was all that I needed to live. She gave me a meaning to live, she gave me a meaning to love.

And the other moment, she was not there. To hold my hands and to be by my side. I was, yet again, all alone with her memories beside me. Even today I smile when I remember, "Bye! Hum bye nahi bolte dear. Itna Jaldi kaise chor denge aapko."

An expensive bed that fails to offer a sound sleep isn't worth it.

"We sat on the stairs in front of my room. There was no one other than us present there. We talked of how I used to sit there and see her.

"Why don't you come to mine?" I don't understand what she means but I don't bother to ask her.

Her mesmerizing voice has its own charm. But she suddenly says that she has to go.

"Why?" I ask in desperate voice, I don't want her to go now. I was enjoying her company.

She stands from where she is sitting.

"Wait here I am coming in a moment." I say her as I went inside to bring the ring I had bought for her. It was the best opportunity and I was not going to let it go.

As I took the ring in my hands, I hear her scream. I rush to her. The ring falls on the floor and breaks. Simran lies there on the ground. She is bleeding."

"No" I scream as I woke from my dream. "Had I not left her, it would have not happened. Had I not left her, she would have never slipped. Had I not left her…"

What does this dream mean? I was sweating heavily as I gained consciousness.

"Come here. She needs you." Sitanshu said from the other side, worried.

The bigger pain is the sedative for smaller pains.
That's one good thing about it.

"What happened?" I ask on the call. Sitanshu doesn't reply. In that time of the night, no one is present on the road. The dying sounds of street dogs is the only live sound that I hear.

"What do mean by nothing?" I speak in nervousness as Sitanshu left the call.

The chilling winds of the night touch my face gently and the only thing that I remember then is Simran doing so. My bike creases to stop as I reach the hospital Sitanshu mentioned.

"As I promised dear, I am here. With you." I spoke to her as the tears dripped from my face. "Now you must keep your promise and we would cherish the moment together."

Simran met a car accident that night. It left me shocked as the doctors said it was a serious case.

I sat beside her, holding her hands for two days in that ICU. I would always ask, "Would my little angel be back for me? Or is she going to punish me for what I did?" And then I broke into tears. Sitanshu kept coming. He took me my meals and left. I knew he was not having the courage to face her.

Those moments I convinced myself, yet again with my favorite story. 'Meera had woken up, my Simran would too.'

And then I held something. I started again, my promise,

"I just want you to remember me when you are alone, so that I may help you with that loneliness. I just want you to remember me when you are sad, so that I may share that sadness with you. I just want you to remember me when you are depressed, so that I may share the load that your heart has to carry, so that I may lighten your heart. I want you to remember me when you shed a tear, so that I may break a smile on your lips from the tear drop. I just want this from you and nothing else." I sat by her side, holding her hands in mine. Her hands feel hot against my cold palm. She is in sleep with her high temperature when my cold tears fall on her forehead. I don't know even if she hears me but I continue, "I am here and I promise I would always be by your side, in all the ups and downs of your life."

Some of the greatest lessons of life are in its tragedy.

That day, she again taught me something. She taught me the real meaning of life and love.

She taught me how it hurts when someone you love the most, lies in front of you in an ICU and you are helpless. She taught me what it feels to crave for your beloved one. She taught me what it means, "God." We remember God when we need him and either plead him or curse. She taught me to do none. I said to him nothing.

I knew Simran was there, hearing me and even the God could not take her away. She taught me what the power of love was.

That afternoon, I kissed her on her forehead and left the room for the first time. I told Sitanshu to sit beside her. I told him to hold her hands.

I left the hospital. Simran knew I was there but she never asked of me again. She knew I was always there with her. She smiled every time, the way she did earlier, to make me see her smile. She taught me something that I could have never learnt. Now I never wonder, what it means to love. Now, I never inter a debate on love. I know what it means.

Simran was true in my dream. Even though, she was not with me, a part of her life was always me. I know she always wished a Good Night to me, deep from her heart. I know she always held something behind her, that we could never know. My dear Simran.

Living in denial won't let you move on.
Acceptance will.

Every day, she comes in my dreams. I still smile in my dream and still remember her.

I still feel the guilt that I left her. I still feel that she would be waiting for me.

Many days, I drive to the lawn in front of our library. I am always hurt to find the place silent. The grounds are there, the walls are there, but they no more hear us there. I am always disappointed not to find Simran there, waiting for me.

Every day, I think that she would be waiting for me. Even though I know she is not, I drive there again. And am left disappointed again.

Some days when I can't help myself, I call my friend, Sitanshu. He tells me about her. I ask more about them. Even though, I hear everything that happened with me, I love them. There is always some things that miss in his telling, the time we enjoyed like a kid.

We were not only lovers, our relationship was different, special. Some days we were the best friends, some days we were love birds, some days we were like brother and sister, and the other days, we were busy pulling each other's leg.

I still shed tears for her. I still hold her photos in my hands. The thing that I missed in them were that I was never seen with her. We never had been together in one of those photographs but…

One sided love stories have their own charm. If only one can learn not to expect.

I sit in the same café where I left everything. In a corner, my seat showed the most beautiful views of outside. It was a beautiful sunset. Very few people occupied the space in the café. I was there after a long time, for some meaning.

They came there and sat in front of me. It looks wonderful to see someone beside her, where I used to be. They too are enjoying the sunset. I had advised Sitanshu to do.

The glass of the café separated us. It felt delighted to see her with her love.

I smile. I saw my promise come true. “My little angel is there, with her love. She would never be left alone.”

I remember the day when she opened her imagination of sitting with Ansh. I laugh.

“Now imagine, what the next?” I speak to myself.

I don’t want to see what she imagined next. I just turn around. My heart felt light. I left the café again, without my Simran with me, but her beautiful thoughts and memories.

Really, one sided love stories have their own charm.

Whenever you think of giving up, think all that you have done for it till then. It'll all be a waste.

And what experience doesn't bring with itself is a fresh perspective to look at things.

In the end, nothing will bother us more that the things we wanted to do & the quarrels we wanted to undo.

I can't change my past, but definitely my perspective to look after it.

Just because it happened in the past doesn't mean that it will happen in the future as well. You can change the course.

I never knew when I slept there. Wondering and thinking about that past, is in itself an adventure. Now, even when I am awake, I chose to keep my eyes close. The winds that gently touched me and flew, reminded me of Simran.

It is the place. The walls would be seeing me, the walls that saw us years ago.

The sunlight above plays with the clouds as we used to play together. I press my eyes when the Sun shines directly above me. It reminds me of Simran, her cute child-like activities.

I smile with the tears in my eyes. I don't care to wipe them, as they hold those beautiful moments, the beautiful words that I exchanged with my little angel.

And then, the sunlight falling from above is blocked, but not by the clouds. This time, the gentle touch is not of the winds. Nor, did the touch flew away. It persists.

I chose not to open my eyes. It seems to be a dream but I enjoy the touch. I don't want to open my eyes to be disappointed again.

"And then, I imagine you in place of him, kissing me deep, in my heart." Our tears mixed together. As I opened my eyes, the beautiful dream did not break. Rather, I had my little angel. She bent forward. Simran…

Absence makes the heart grow fonder.

Acknowledgements:

I am indebted towards my family, my younger brother specially.

I should not forget my publishing team that regarded my work.

Luck to have Ravinder Singh with his quotes to carve my life and my work. Savi Sharma's inspirational and motivation words were also there always to help me. They really touched my heart.

At last, than you all for being a part of my work, for enjoying this. Hope we would be meeting again, in a new piece of writing.

Printed by Libri Plureos GmbH in Hamburg,
Germany